MAX

MAX

story & pictures by
Rachel Isadora

MACMILLAN PUBLISHING CO., INC.
New York
COLLIER MACMILLAN PUBLISHERS
London

Macmillan Publishing Co., Inc.

866 Third Avenue, New York, N.Y. 10022

Collier Macmillan Canada, Ltd.

Printed in the United States of America

10   9   8   7   6   5   4   3   2   1

Library of Congress Cataloging in Publication Data

Isadora, Rachel.
 Max.

SUMMARY: Max finds a new way to warm up for his Saturday baseball game—his sister's dancing class.
 [1. Dancing—Fiction.   2. Baseball—Fiction]
I. Title.
PZ7.I763Max   [E]   76-9088
ISBN 0-02-747450-7

For my parents
and Grandfather Max

With special thanks to
Libby, Alan,
and of course, Brian

Max is a great baseball player. He can run fast, jump high, and hardly ever misses a ball. Every Saturday he plays with his team in the park.

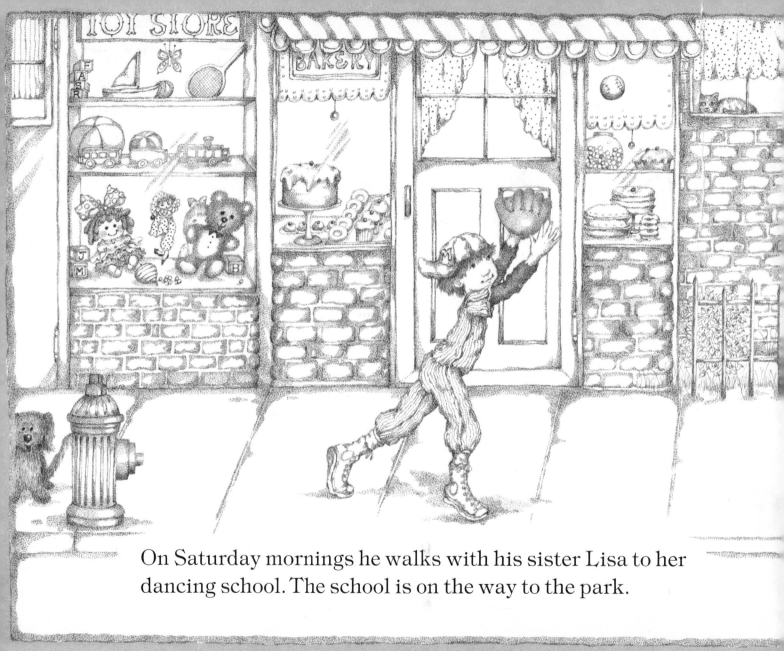

On Saturday mornings he walks with his sister Lisa to her dancing school. The school is on the way to the park.

One Saturday when they reach the school, Max still has lots of time before the game is to start. Lisa asks him if he wants to come inside for a while.

Max doesn't really want to, but he says O.K. Soon the class begins. He gets a chair and sits near the door to watch.

The teacher invites Max
to join the class, but he must
take off his sneakers first.

He stretches at the barre.

He tries to do the split.

And the pas de chat. He is having fun.

Just as the class lines up to do leaps across the floor,
Lisa points to the clock. It is time for Max to leave.

Max doesn't want to miss the leaps. He waits
and takes his turn.

Then he must go.

He leaps all the way to the park.

He is late. Everybody is waiting for him.

He goes up to bat.

Strike one!

He tries again.

Strike two!

And then...

A home run!

Now Max has a new way to warm up for the game on Saturdays.
He goes to dancing class.

E   ISADORA: Max.

DATE DUE   6.85.

JY 15 '85	SE 8 '86	FE 5 '90	JU 2 9 '93
JY 17 '85	JE 20 '87	AUG 30 1991	NOV 3 9 '93
AG 7 '85	JY 15 '87	OCT 4 1991	
SE 7 '85	JY 27 '87	NOV 15 1991	
SE 23 '85	FE 24 '88	FEB 7 1992	
C 21 '85	MR 14 '88	FEB 21 1992	
NO 23 '85	AG 10 '88	JUL 15 1992	
FE 5 '86	NO 23 '88	JUL 25 1992	
MR 24 '86	JA 30 '89	AUG 29 1992	
JE 7 '86	JE 7 '89	NOV 13 1992	
JY 16 '86	AG 2 '89	JUL 21 199	
AG 4 '86	OC 4 '89	DEC 3 1 199	
AG 20 '86	NO 17 '89	FEB 13 199	

GAYLORD   PRINTED IN U.S.A.